W9-BSQ-970

Dear Parents and Educators,

Welcome to Penguin Young Readers! As parents and educators, you know that each child develops at his or her own pace—in terms of speech, critical thinking, and, of course, reading. Penguin Young Readers recognizes this fact. As a result, each Penguin Young Readers book is assigned a traditional easy-to-read level (1–4) as well as a Guided Reading Level (A–P). Both of these systems will help you choose the right book for your child. Please refer to the back of each book for specific leveling information. Penguin Young Readers features esteemed authors and illustrators, stories about favorite characters, fascinating nonfiction, and more!

A Pig, a Fox, and a Box

LEVEL **2**

GUIDED READING LEVEL **H**

This book is perfect for a **Progressing Reader** who:
• can figure out unknown words by using picture and context clues;
• can recognize beginning, middle, and ending sounds;
• can make and confirm predictions about what will happen in the text; and
• can distinguish between fiction and nonfiction.

Here are some **activities** you can do during and after reading this book:
• Picture Clues: Use the pictures to tell the story. Have the child go through the book, retelling the story just by looking at the pictures.
• Make Predictions: At the end of this story, Fox is finished tricking Pig for the day. Do you think Fox will try to trick Pig again tomorrow? What do you think he will do?

Remember, sharing the love of reading with a child is the best gift you can give!

—Bonnie Bader, EdM
   Penguin Young Readers program

*Penguin Young Readers are leveled by independent reviewers applying the standards developed by Irene Fountas and Gay Su Pinnell in *Matching Books to Readers: Using Leveled Books in Guided Reading*, Heinemann, 1999.

For Chad, Christopher, Amanda,
Michael, Katie, and Gregory.
Fine siblings all—JF

PENGUIN YOUNG READERS
Published by the Penguin Group
Penguin Group (USA) LLC, 375 Hudson Street, New York, New York 10014, USA

USA | Canada | UK | Ireland | Australia | New Zealand | India | South Africa | China

penguin.com
A Penguin Random House Company

Library of Congress Control Number: 2014044337

ISBN 978-0-448-48510-2 (pbk)   10 9 8 7 6 5 4 3 2 1
ISBN 978-0-448-48511-9 (hc)   10 9 8 7 6 5 4 3 2

A PIG, A FOX, AND A BOX

by Jonathan Fenske

Penguin Young Readers
An Imprint of Penguin Group (USA) LLC

PART ONE

5

Oh, Pig, come here!
Oh, Pig, come see!

Did I just hear
Fox call for me?

PART TWO

I put the wig under the rocks . . .

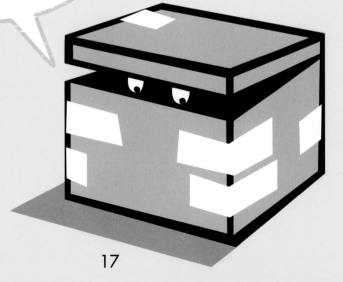

and hide inside my little box.

Help, help, big Pig!
Oh help!
Come see!

Did I just hear
Fox call for me?

That big, big pile of heavy rocks was on a wig, not on a fox.

Help, help, big Pig!
Oh help!
Come see!
There is a pile of rocks on me!

PART THREE